TAKE IT OR LEAVE IT

The First (Complete) Play by Sam Maistros

Special Thanks To:

The CSA Drama Department

Steve and Katy Maistros

Ms. Telich

Dr. Miller

And so many more!

Cast

Pat: a headstrong, unstoppable inspector

Henry: a nervous kid who was adopted into the orphanage from parents in a bad situation

Zaglis: a heartless villain who wants her own, infinite comfort and will get it by any means necessary

Ms. Verwerp: a kind woman who tried to build the orphanage for righteous goals but was betrayed by Zaglis and was locked in a safe for four years

Kids:

Twitchy

Draco

Krunchy Krab

Shadow

Pinhead

Beat Box

Peaches

Stutter Box

Gummy Braces

Obese Whale

Chico Stick

Bugs

Sticky Pop

Bactoria

Toothless

Yeast Infection

Goneria (not pronounced like the STD)

SCENE I

(We open up on all the kids in the orphanage except Henry causing chaos. a group of them are throwing paper balls at each other)

(Henry enters walking to center stage in a slow and exasperated way)

(Henry reaches center stage and everything freezes)

HENRY: Dear diary, I don't think there's anything worse than this orphanage and if there is it has to be some kind of hell. Everyone seems to have this intense fascination with torturing me.

(Unfreeze and the kids cause more chaos)

(A few seconds pass and they freeze again one of them has their arm on Henry)

HENRY: SEE?! It's not even like Ms. Zaglis is helping, in fact, I feel like she's making everything worse. Like, she may be causing all my suffering. Directly, and indirectly.

(Unfreeze)

(Freeze again)

HENRY: I mean, I would be fine with it if this place was actually a nice place to stay, but it's not. I've had to rename the cockroaches every day this week cause Ms. Zaglis keeps forgetting that I named them the day before. I feel like one of these days I'm gonna break.

(Unfreeze)

(The chaos continues for a couple of seconds then Zaglis enters)

(When they don't notice her she blows a whistle and then they notice)

(They run around cleaning everything up then line up facing the audience army style)

(Zaglis walks down the line with a trash can and each of the kids throws away the paper balls they've hidden on their person)

(Zaglis paces down the line as she scolds the kids)

ZAGLIS: You kids are obviously too young to know anything about death. Cause if you did THE CAT WOULDN'T BE MISSING IT'S MOUSE TOY! Now if the person who committed this horrible act would step forward I promise that I won't strangle them too much.

HENRY: Permission to speak ma'am.

ZAGLIS: You don't even have permission to speak about asking to speak Henry, shut up.

HENRY: Yes ma'am.

TWITCHY: Permission to speak ma'am.

ZAGLIS: Go ahead Twitchy.

TWITCHY: That was not a toy ma'am that was an actual mouse. The cat killed it Last week and it was starting to smell really bad so someone threw it out.

(There is a tense pause as Zaglis considers how to respond)

ZAGLIS: I would be angry, but honestly I would probably do the same thing.

TWITCHY: T-t-thank you man

(The kids breathe a sigh of relief)

ZAGLIS: But don't think you little twerps are off the hook just yet.

(They all tense up again)

ZAGLIS: All of the most important chores aren't even done yet. And by pure coincidence, there's one job for each of you.

(She goes to the front of the line and gives each kid a job)

ZAGLIS: Draco.

(Draco steps forward)

DRACO: Yes ma'am.

ZAGLIS: Polish the lightbulbs.

DRACO: Thank you, ma'am.

(Draco steps back)

ZAGLIS: Krunchy Krab.

(Krunchy Krab steps forward)

KRUNCHY KRAB: Yes ma'am.

ZAGLIS: Mop the ceiling.

KRUNCHY KRAB: Thank you, ma'am.

(Krunchy Krab steps back)

ZAGLIS: Shadow.

(Shadow steps forward)

SHADOW: Yes ma'am.

ZAGLIS: Milk the guinea pig.

SHADOW: Thank you, ma'am.

(Shadow steps back)

ZAGLIS: Stutter Box.

(Stutter Box steps forward)

STUTTER BOX: Yes ma'am.

ZAGLIS: Brush my wigs.

STUTTER BOX: Thank you, ma'am.
(Stutter Box steps back)

ZAGLIS: Pinhead.

(Pinhead steps forward)

PINHEAD: Yes ma'am

ZAGLIS: Pluck my nose hairs… I'll… talk to you…. Later.

PINHEAD: Thank you, ma'am.

(Pinhead steps back)

ZAGLIS: Gummy Braces.

(Gummy Braces steps forward)

GUMMY BRACES: Yes ma'am.

ZAGLIS: Oil the windows.

GUMMY BRACES: Thank you, ma'am.

(Gummy Braces steps back)

ZAGLIS: Beat Box.

(Wrinkles steps forward)

BEATBOX: Yes ma'am.

ZAGLIS: Clean the chimney.

BEATBOX: Thank you, ma'am.

(Beat Box steps back)

ZAGLIS: Obese Whale.

(Obese Whale steps forward)

OBESE WHALE: Yes ma'am.

ZAGLIS: Wash the fish.

OBESE WHALE: Thank you, ma'am.

(Obese Whale steps back)

ZAGLIS: Chico Stick.

(Chico Stick steps forward)

CHICO STICK: Yes ma'am.

ZAGLIS: Color coordinate and alphabetize my socks.

CHICO STICK: Thank you, ma'am.

(Chico Stick steps back)

ZAGLIS: Leo.

(Leo steps forward)

BUGS: Yes ma'am.

ZAGLIS: Braid the carpet.

BUGS: Thank you, ma'am.

(Bugs steps back)

ZAGLIS: Sticky Pop.

(Sticky Pop steps forward)

STICKY POP: Yes ma'am.

ZAGLIS: Vacuum the walls.

STICKY POP: Thank you, ma'am.

(Sticky Pop steps back)

ZAGLIS: Bactoria.

(Bactoria steps forward)

BACTORIA: Yes ma'am.

ZAGLIS: Floss the cat.

BACTORIA: Thank you, ma'am.

(Bactoria steps back)

ZAGLIS: Toothless,

(Toothless steps forward)

TOOTHLESS: Yes ma'am.

ZAGLIS: Polish the toothbrushes.

TOOTHLESS: Yes ma'am.

(Toothless steps back)

ZAGLIS: Yeast Infection.

(Yeast infection steps forward)

YEAST INFECTION: Yes ma'am.

ZAGLIS: Burn the garbage disposal.

YEAST INFECTION: Thank you, ma'am.

(Yeast Infection steps back)

ZAGLIS: Goneria.

GONERIA: Yes ma'am.

ZAGLIS: Organize my pills.

GONERIA: Shampoo the cups.

ZAGLIS: Henry.

(Henry steps forward)

HENRY: Yes ma'am.

ZAGLIS: Name the cockroaches.

HENRY: But I did that yesterday- I mean um uh!

(All the kids step back)

ZAGLIS: So Henry, do you like it here?

HENRY: Yes ma'am

ZAGLIS: Are you sure?

HENRY: YES MA'AM YES YOU'RE THE GREATEST CHILDCARE PERSON OF ALL TIME!

(Zaglis grabs the trash can and shoves it on his head)

ZAGLIS: HEY HEY HENRY DO YOU LIKE IT HERE HUH?! HUH?!

HENRY: YES!

ZAGLIS: LOUDER!

(Silence)

ZAGLIS: ANSWER ME, YOU PIGEON BREATHED YELLOW TOOTH, YOU CONSTIPATED SEA BASS LOOKIN, YOU'RE AS GRACEFUL AS A FLY ON A WINDSHIELD, YOU HEXAGON HEADED SLIME BALL OF A CHILD YOU'RE AS DUMB AS A DROWNING GOLDFISH, CALLING YOU AN IDIOT WOULD BE INSULTING TO ALL STUPID PEOPLE, STUPIDITY IS NOT A CRIME SO YOU ARE FREE TO GO MY FRIEND, I FEEL LIKE YOU HAVE A TERRIBLE EMPTY FEELING IN YOUR SKULL, IN FAC-

(The doorbell rings, interrupting her)

(Zaglis looks off stage annoyed)

(she glares at Henry with the trash can on his head)

ZAGLIS: No one move, I'm gonna talk to our visitor for a second, you know shoo them away. Then we'll finish *this.*

(Zaglis starts to exit then pauses)

ZAGLIS: Also, cause of this *(she gestures towards Henry)* twerp none of you are getting any food today, so don't get any bright ideas.

(She stomps off stage)

(All the kids glare at Henry as he whimpers and the lights dim just before we see what happens yet)

SCENE II

(Sally enters)

ZAGLIS: Hello welcome to take it or leave it adoption center where we love children *almost* as much as we love money.

(Zaglis laughs but Sally isn't laughing)

ZAGLIS: My name is Zaglis how may I help.

SALLY: Hello, my name is Sally Montgomery I'm from the Snotty Nosed Organization for protection of kids or S.N.O.K for short. I'm here for an-

ZAGLIS: *(sarcastic)* Excuse me, did you say snot?

SALLY: SNok

ZAGLIS: Slop?

SALLY: Snok

ZAGLIS: Schnapps?

SALLY: Snok!

ZAGLIS: Snorkel?

SALLY: I said SNOK!

ZAGLIS: Spell it out.

SALLY: S-N-O-K

ZAGLIS: That would be snook wouldn't it?

SALLY: *ANYWAY,* one of your old kids Jacob, and others sources have given us stories of abus-

ZAGLIS: Oh, he was dropped on his head as a baby.

SALLY: Well did you drop him.

ZAGLIS: It was an acci- I mean why would you assume that I love those kids.

SALLY: To get straight to the point I'd like to meet the children.

ZAGLIS: Oh, I don't think that would work right now they're..... Napping.

SALLY: Well, can't you just wake them up.

ZAGLIS: Well, if I wake one up they'll all wake up and I'll have to deal with all of them, you know kids.

SALLY: Oh, of course, I have all the time in the world.

ZAGLIS: *(she growls to herself)* Ok listen I'm gonna have to ask you to leave, it's just too inconvenient of a time, maybe we can reschedule, I mean your visit was, unexpected at best and rude at worst.

SALLY: Well then I assume you will have some other time available that we can do an interview and maybe even a tour, all of my time is free generally always since no one wants to give me an assignment since and I am She's snotty and non-negotiable" So I will have this meeting with you at any day month time or year same with the interview. So *there.*

ZAGLIS: *(to an audience member)* Damn she's aggressive and persistent.

SALLY: So what'll it be?

ZAGLIS: Heh heh *no.*

(As Sally says this next line we watch Zaglis slowly shrink as she panics)

SALLY: Fine I'll just get my superiors down here and they'll search this place themselves probably get it shut down in the process, or worse of all, you could go to prison.

ZAGLIS: Y-y-yes that makes sense. O-oh would you look at the time their nap time just ended I'll go wake them up.

(Sally takes out her phone and makes a call)

SALLY: Hello Bob, yes I'm getting access to the children right now *(to Zaglis)* I'll take this outside.

(Pat exits)

(Zaglis blows her whistle)

(The kids rush in and line up chaotically)

ZAGLIS: O-ok kids there's a lady out there. A *very* scary lady. She's gonna ask you some questions. You're gonna lie to her face. If any of you tell any piece of the truth I *will* throttle you. If any of you break the last thing you will ever see is the look of fury in my eyes or the pavement rushing at you as you fall off the top of a building to your death. Arrrgggghhh and- and JUST LISTEN BAD THINGS WILL HAPPEN IF YOU TWERPS SCREW THIS UP!! NONE OF YOU WILL BE

FED UNTIL YOU'RE AS OLD AS I AM. I SWEAR ON MY
INTERNET HISTORY IF YOU GUYS EXPOSE THIS
PLACE YOU'LL WISH YOU WERE NEVER BORN!

(Pinhead raises his head)

PINHEAD: Did you just promise to show us your internet
history if we lied good.

ZAGLIS: Absolutely not.

(Sally enters)

SALLY: Ah, these must be the children.

ZAGLIS: Yep look at all their happy faces. *(She glares at the
kids and they all smile)*

SALLY: Yes they all seem quite happy.

(There is an awkward silence)

SALLY: *(she gestures towards Zaglis)* you can leave now.

ZAGLIS: What do you mean Sally?

SALLY: Well, I can't interview the children while you're
here.

ZAGLIS: Why not I think the kids would feel more
comfortable if I was here.

SALLY: I *highly* doubt that.

SALLY: Zaglis, please leave.

ZAGLIS: ...*Fine.* Kids remember my interview advice, I'll be right outside... outside... the door.

(All the kids shudder)

(Zaglis exits)

SALLY: So kids I'm going to ask you some questions, obviously. I want you to answer truthfully and to the best of your abilities. You first. *(She points to Ghonoria)* what's your name?

GHONORIA: Ghonoria.

SALLY: *Oh boy.* So is that your actual name or are you just called that?

GHONORIA: As far as I know that is my name.

SALLY: OK NEW PERSON. You *(she points at obese whale)* what's your name?

OBESE WHALE: Obese Whale.

SALLY: Oh boy, I guess it's better than the name Goneria we'll go with that. What do you think of this orphanage just as a whole?

OBESE WHALE: Oh I love it here Ms. Zaglis is wonderful and is kind to us, as you saw ma'am.

SALLY: *(sarcastically)* Yes, I could really feel her kind soul emanating from her.

OBESE WHALE: Yes it's our own personal slice of heaven.

SALLY: Ok next child. You *(she points at Henry)* what's your name?

HENRY: Henry.

SALLY: Oh thank god.

HENRY: Aren't you supposed to ask me questions?

SALLY: Be patient! If you could describe this place in one word what would it be?

HENRY: *(Henry answers a bit too fast)* perfect.

SALLY: *(skeptical)* Ok. What do you think of Zaglis?

HENRY: Delightfully helpful.

SALLY: Ok, what about your living space.

HENRY: I-I-I-It's v-very co-comfy.

SALLY: Are you sure?

HENRY: NO THIS IS LITERALLY THE WORST PLACE THAT HAS EVER EXISTED EVERY DAY THE PRESSURE OF HAVING TO DEAL WITH THE UNSTOPPABLE PULL TOWARDS INSANITY AS MS. ZAGLIS AND THESE BUTTHOLES TORTURE AND ABUSE ME. THEY ALL SLOWLY TEAR APART MY SELF ESTEEM AS I THINK THAT EVERYTHING IS MY FAULT! DON'T EVEN GET ME STARTED ON MS. ZAGLIS' TREATMENT OF ALL OF US! I'VE HAD TO RENAME THE COCKROACHES ALL WEEK!

(The kids give Henry a long stare and start to intimidatingly inch towards him then as Henry inches back he runs into Shadow)

(Shadow puts his hand on Henry's shoulder)

SHADOW: Where do you think you're going?

GHONORIA: KICK HIS HEINIE!

(All the kids charge and lift up Henry screaming)

(Ms. Zaglis blows her whistle)

ZAGLIS: Kids *put him down.*

(They put Henry down)

SALLY: Well I thank you, I have enough information.

ZAGLIS: Wait, *(to the children)* children. *(she gestures towards the door)*

(All the kids block the exit)

ZAGLIS: It seems we have a situation here. You have something I don't want anyone to know, and if you leave you'll tell everyone. So the simple answer is that you don't leave.

SALLY: This is outrageous, barbaric, my superiors will be here as soon as I make this- *(she attempts to take out her phone but it isn't there)* where is my phone?

(Shadow pulls Sally's phone out, dangles it in front of his face)

SALLY: How did you do that?!

SHADOW: They don't call me shadow for nothing.

(Sally says nothing, defeated)

ZAGLIS: Now Henry.

HENRY: Y-y-y-es m-m-m-ma'am.

ZAGLIS: I never knew you felt that way, I'm sorry, *(she waves Henry towards her)* come here. *(Zaglis holds Henry in a hug)* it must've been hard holding in all those angry emotions. I believe there's only one thing we can do in this situation.

HENRY: W-w-what?

ZAGLIS: *(she grabs his face and puts it close to hers)* THE SAFE!

HENRY: OH GODDDD NOT THE SAFE!

ZAGLIS: In fact, you kids have never seen the safe before, have you?

(All the kids shake their heads.)

ZAGLIS: Well, let's take a field trip.

(The kids all pick up Henry or drag Sally off stage with Zaglis leading the way)

SCENE III

(The scene changes to a room with two benches and Ms. Verwerp sitting on one of them)

(Zaglis enters)

(Zaglis pauses and gives Verwerp a look of distaste)

ZAGLIS: *Verwerp.*

VERWERP: Ah, Zaglis it's been quite a while, hasn't it?

ZAGLIS: Quite.

VERWERP: You look good.

ZAGLIS: You *don't.*

VERWERP: *(sarcastically)* Really? I wonder why? Maybe, and this is just a small thought, it's because I've been locked in this safe for an uncertain amount of time, to me at least, with only bread and water to get by.

ZAGLIS: You now Verwerp, you always aggravated m-

VERWERP: Oh please, let's be honest with ourselves, you're scared of me.

ZAGLIS: I-I-I-I d-don't know what you're talking about.

VERWERP: I'm the only one who can get in your head and you know it, and you know why I can because I understand your pain and I dealt with that pain better than you ever could n-

ZAGLIS: ENOUGH WITH THE GAMES VERWERP! *(She calms down)* I have some company for you.

HENRY: Hi...

VERWERP: Ah well that's good, cabin fever was obviously my problem

ZAGLIS: Well, I hope you three enjoy each other's company until the day you die.

(Zaglis leaves)

VERWERP: *(to Henry)* What are *you* doing in here?

HENRY: I ratted out on Zaglis

VERWERP: Did you now?

SALLY: Yes, *(Sally steps forward)* hello, my name is Sally Montgomery I'm from the Snotty Nosed Organization for protection of kids or S.N.-

(Verwerp suddenly gets really excited)

VERWERP: OH MY GOD YOU'RE FROM S.N.O.K!

SALLY: Yeah that's what I wa-

VERWERP: DO YOU NEED STORIES?!

SALLY: I feel like I'm gonna get them either way.

VERWERP: I watched Zaglis trap one of the kids in a refrigerator.

24

HENRY: Oh yeah, I remember that was Peaches.

VERWERP: She forced them to eat pancakes with mustard.

HENRY: That day has haunted my nightmares for years.

VERWERP: She made them cut the grass with their teeth.

HENRY: No wait *that's* the day that haunts my nightmares.

VERWERP: She switched shampoo with dog feces.

(Henry gags)

VERWERP: She forced them to eat 20 hardboiled eggs in 30 minutes.

HENRY: Not as hard as it sounds.

VERWERP: She had them stick their underwear in the freezer for three hours than have to wear it.

HENRY: That was just absurd.

VERWERP: She had them wear a face mask with sardine juice.

HENRY: And she only told us afterword.

SALLY: How did you not notice you were wearing a face mask with sardine juice?

HENRY: WE WERE YOUNG SALLY!

VERWERP: After seeing all of this I decided that I was tired of it, I loved those kids and I was gonna defend them, so I tried to leave for the police. Unfortunately, Zaglis caught me that night and locked me in here.

HENRY: Wait, Zaglis told us you told her that you hated us, and that's why you left.

VERWERP: No I was trying to save you guys from her.

HENRY: Well you, didn't do a very good job of that, did you?

VERWERP: No Henry, I really didn't, and I wish I had I can't imagine what you and the other kids have gone through under her. I've missed you kids like hell

SALLY: Well, we've got to reunite you with those kids, how are we getting out of here?

VERWERP: I have no idea, I've searched this place in and… in, trying to find any weak points within this structure with no luck. I don't know how long I've been in here but it's been long enough for me to have at least found something, but nothing.

SALLY: Well then we can look for other, more outward sources of escape.

HENRY: Why should we, she'll just lock us in here again and crush our spirits, none of us were able to get out of here on our own so how could all of us get out of here. When you multiply zero by itself three times you still get zero. We are destined to fail.

(Henry sits on one of the benches and cups his face in his head)

(After a moment Verwerp sits down next to Henry)

VERWERP: Do you remember what the orphanage was like when I co-ran it with Zaglis.

HENRY: Honestly, no.

VERWERP: Oh, well I guess you didn't want to remember our time together after being told that I secretly hated you the whole time and had left you to live under the "care" of Zaglis, but this place could be so much more than a place of scarred young minds, it can be perfect it can be a home for all those abandoned, like us.

(Henry still says nothing)

VERWERP: And if it helps, I'm sorry.

HENRY: *(he looks up at Verwerp)* No, that won't help, I want you to admit that you failed. I think that'll make up for what we've been through, and if you don't think so, we have our whole lives to figure this out.

VERWERP: I would admit to my greatest crime to save you, kids, so yes I failed, I let you down and in the process destroyed your opinion of me. I am sorry.

(Henry looks at Verwerp for a second then gives her a hug)

HENRY: I'm sorry Verwerp, it's been a tough time, I missed you

VERWERP: I missed you too, now let's get out of here.

(They break their hug)

HENRY: I may have an idea.

VERWERP: Shoot.

HENRY: Do you know who delivers you your bread and water?

VERWERP: Two kids, one has a scratchy voice and the other sounds really stupid.

HENRY: I knew there was always something missing in the morning. So the kids who are delivering you food are named Shadow and Pinhead by Ms. Zaglis, Shadow is something that isn't human that suddenly appeared a couple years ago, but importantly he has a hoodie he never takes off and pinhead is an idiot, so if we can find a way to get shadow inside I can sneak out in his hoodie, the only problem is how to lure Shadow in here without Pinhead.

SALLY: We could pretend I'm having a heart attack.

VERWERP: Perfect!

(There is an awkward silence)

SALLY: So we wait now.

(There's a knock on the door)

PINHEAD: Stand away from the door. I have your food.

HENRY: Everybody ready?

PINHEAD: You away from the door? Don't try nothing funny. Shadow is right here next to me and he'll call Zaglis if you try anything.

HENRY: We're away from the door. Come on in.

(Pinhead enters with a tray of food)

HENRY: Hey Pinhead, did you know all along Verwerp was in here?

PINHEAD: Maybe. I don't know. I don't know nothing 'bout nobody, no-how.

(Pinhead starts to leave. Henry signals to Sally)

HENRY: Go on… Go on…

SALLY: Oh, right.

(Sally pretends to have a heart attack. Henry motions for her to exaggerate it.)

PINHEAD: What's wrong with her?

HENRY: She's having a heart attack.

PINHEAD: A fart attack?

HENRY: Not a fart attack. A heart attack. Do something!

PINHEAD: Like what?

HENRY: Get Shadow in here.

PINHEAD: He's outside the door.

HENRY: I know he's outside the door. Get him in here.

PINHEAD: But he's supposed to stay outside the door.

HENRY: She's going to die. Get Shadow in here. Now!

PINHEAD: Okay. (Calls) Shadow!

SHADOW: (Outside the door) What?

PINHEAD: Come in here.

HENRY: (To Pinhead) Tell him to hurry.

PINHEAD: Hurry.

(Shadow enters. *Henry jumps on his back knocking Shadow out. Henry puts on Shadow's hoodie.*)

HENRY: Pinhead, you wait here.

PINHEAD: Okay.

HENRY: Let's move!

(They exit out the safe door)

PINHEAD: *(a pause for realization) Wait* a minute…

SCENE IV

(The protagonists run through the halls.)

HENRY: Follow me, I know a back exit.

(The three protagonists run to the back door.

HENRY: It's locked. Over here.

(They run to another door.)

HENRY: It's also locked. Come on.

(They run to a third door. Shadow enters.)

SALLY: Oh my God how did you do that?!

SHADOW: They don't call me Shadow for nothing.

(They run to another exit. Goneria enters.)

GONERIA PEACHES: Well, well, well if it isn't Henry ... and... you two....

HENRY: Didn't Sally introduce herself yesterday?

GONERIA: I assumed I would never see her again.

SALLY: You know what, that's fair.

GONERIA: Now Henry, do you know how happy Ms. Zaglis would be with us if we brought you back to her.

HENRY: In your mind at least, if you bring us to Zaglis nothing will change, you'll still suffer, you'll just suffer without me. She won't spare you. But if you let us run we can fix ever-

GONERIA: You've done enough.

(Goneria makes a sound. All the other kids enter.)

GONERIA: Grab them.

(The kids begin to charge in but Henry interrupts them)

HENRY: WAAAAAAAAAAIIIIIIIIITTTTTTTTT!

ZAGLIS: What are you doing?

HENRY: Before you all tear us to pieces, I have one more thing to say. If you'll let me.

GONERIA: Fine, but just one more thing.

HENRY: Zaglis lied to us!

(The kids react)

GONERIA: Wait, Wait, Wait, what did she lie about?

HENRY: She lied about Verwerp, you remember her right? *(the kids nod)* well, she didn't hate us, she didn't even leave she was in the safe the whole time and she's right there *(Henry gestures towards Verwerp).*

(the kids react)

HENRY: Come on, Verwerp reminded me what this place almost was and what it still could be. We can revolt. *(the kids seem skeptical)*

VERWERP: Please kids you can do this, you are strong, I want you to be free from her torture, get past your fears and fight back against her, please if you won't do it for me, do it for yourselves. Please, I'll do my best to make you happy jus-

(Zaglis bursts in the room dragging Pinhead by his ear)

ZAGLIS: Well, well, well. Look who I found, Sally, Henry, and Verwerp. Kids, grab them.

(The kids won't grab them)

ZAGLIS: A-hem, did you twerps not hear me.

DRACO: Um, ms Zaglis are we gonna eat? I'm really hungry

ZAGLIS: No, you all won't get fed, you just disobeyed me, now grab them

(The kids still don't move)

ZAGLIS: Why, you little backstabbers, working with the enemy, huh you all should be really ashamed of yourselves you all won't be eating i-

BEATBOX: (*struggles to get herself to speak. Eventually says...*) SHUT UP!!

ALL THE KIDS: Yeah. Shut up.

(The kids start to move toward Zaglis.)

ZAGLIS: Wait what are you doing? You twerps have no p-p-powe-. Get back, get back.

(The kids grab her)

(They kids hold Zaglis)

YEAST INFECTION: What should we do to her?

VERWERP: Let's keep her in the safe and wait for the police to show up, then we'll go get Chili's.

(the kids all cheer and drag Zaglis off stage chanting "SAFE...SAFE...SAFE..." as Zaglis yells: "Hey Wait, Verwerp! Let go of me!!!" Everyone leaves except Henry.)

HENRY: Dear Diary, I know it's cliche but everyone ended up happy. Verwerp gained full power over the orphanage. I ended up being adopted by Sally almost immediately after that. We still don't know where Shadow came from but the next day he just up of vanished. I guess we'll never know his secrets. Occasionally I'll think all of the happiness that's come into my life has just been a dream. Then I pinch myself to see if I'm right. Luckily I'm wrong. Or I'm REALLY deep in sleep that would also be a possibility. But if this is a dream, I don't think I want to wake up.

(Everyone enters and begins to dance.)

END OF PLAY